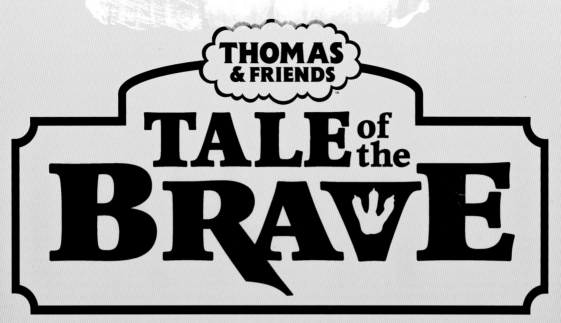

THOMAS & FRIENDS™
TALE of the BRAVE
THE MOVIE STORYBOOK

EGMONT
We bring stories to life

First published in Great Britain 2014
by Egmont UK Limited
The Yellow Building
1 Nicholas Road
London W11 4AN

Thomas the Tank Engine & Friends™

CREATED BY BRITT ALLCROFT

Based on the Railway Series by the Reverend W Awdry
© 2014 Gullane (Thomas) LLC. A HIT Entertainment company.
Thomas the Tank Engine & Friends and Thomas & Friends are
trademarks of Gullane (Thomas) Limited.
Thomas the Tank Engine & Friends and Design is
Reg. U.S. Pat. & Tm. Off.

ISBN 978 1 4052 7312 1
57716/1
Printed in Italy

FSC
MIX
Paper
FSC® C018306

Egmont is passionate about helping to preserve the world's remaining ancient forests.
We only use paper from legal and sustainable forest sources.

This book is made from paper certified by the Forest Stewardship Council® (FSC®),
an organisation dedicated to promoting responsible management of forest resources.
For more information on the FSC, please visit www.fsc.org. To learn more about
Egmont's sustainable paper policy, please visit www.egmont.co.uk/ethical

Stay safe online. Any website addresses listed in this book are correct at the time of
going to print. However, Egmont is not responsible for content hosted by third parties.
Please be aware that online content can be subject to change and websites can contain
content that is unsuitable for children. We advise that all children are supervised when
using the internet.

CHAPTER 1

It was a bright and sunny day on the Island of Sodor. Engines were carrying passengers and goods up and down every line on The Fat Controller's railway . . . except Thomas' branch line. It was closed for repairs.

Thomas **cheerily** made his way to the Clay Pits where he had been sent to pull trucks out of the trenches with Bill and Ben.

"Hello, Thomas," said Ben. "Your trucks are over there."

"Don't be silly, Ben," said Bill. "Thomas isn't strong enough to pull those trucks."

"Of course I am!" cried Thomas, stubbornly. He backed up to be coupled to the trucks.

Thomas started to pull forwards slowly.

"Be careful, Thomas," warned his friend, Timothy. "If a storm comes, the heavy rain can make the clay walls **dangerous**."

Thomas thanked Timothy and headed off through a narrow gully. He struggled through the rain pulling the empty trucks. Lightning lit up the sky and Thomas saw some very big, three-toed footprints on a rock. Thomas whistled with **fright**! Suddenly Bill and Ben pushed him away – just in time to avoid a landslide!

The next day Thomas was supposed to work at the Docks but he wanted to go back to the pits and find out more about the footprints. At the pits he met a steam shovel called Marion, who loved to talk. Thomas asked her if she knew any animals big enough to make those footprints. "**Dinosaurs** were very big animals!" she replied. "But dinosaurs aren't around anymore. No. They lived a very, very, very long time ago."

Thomas thanked her and headed to the Docks. When he arrived his friend Percy asked about the footprints. "Did you find out what made them?" he asked.

"Not yet," replied Thomas. "But they were very big footprints – bigger than any animal on Sodor!"

"You mean they were the footprints of . . . a **monster**?" Percy was **terrified**.

"There's no such thing as monsters. There's no such thing as monsters," repeated Percy nervously to himself as he puffed across the Island. Suddenly he saw a strange shape coming towards him. It looked like a giant alligator's head with a long snaking body, moving along the tracks.

"**Monster! Oh run away, run away!**" screamed Percy.

CHAPTER 2

Percy pulled backwards as fast as he could and raced to the Docks, where Thomas, Cranky and Salty were working. **"A monster! A monster! It's coming this way!"** cried Percy. Thomas looked up to see the alligator-headed thing creeping into the Docks. Cranky panicked, squeezed his eyes shut and dropped the pallet of sand bags he was lifting.

The strangest-looking engine they'd ever seen arrived, pulling a long line of trucks.

"Ha argh, that be no monster, Percy! That be an engine!" said Salty, laughing.

"Hello," said the new engine. "They call me 'Gator'. It's because my long sloping water tank makes me look like an **alligator**!"

Percy felt silly for thinking Gator was a monster but he was still very scared about the giant footprints. As he pulled the Mail Train later that night he started seeing monsters everywhere. The shadow of a **big hairy monster** was by the tracks . . . but as Percy got nearer he saw that it was only a haystack. Then he saw something that looked like a monster waving its arms about . . . but it was only washing on a clothesline.

The next night Percy asked Thomas to do his mail run for him. "Please, Thomas," he pleaded. "Last night I kept seeing things that looked like . . . monsters!"

Thomas was happy to help his friend. But James just teased Percy. "You're such a **scaredy engine**," he said.

The next day Percy puffed to the Docks to work with Salty and Cranky. He was surprised to see Gator there. "Are you working on Sodor now?" Percy asked.

"No, Percy. I missed my ship. I'm just helping the Dock Manager while I wait for the next ship. He needs me to collect some trucks from Duck's branch line tonight," replied Gator.

"Tonight? But . . . aren't you afraid of monsters?"

"**What monsters?**" laughed Gator. "Monsters would probably be afraid of me!"

"I wish I was as **brave** as you are, Gator," said Percy.

"I wasn't always brave . . . " replied Gator.

Gator told Percy a story about when he worked in the mountains and discovered he was afraid of heights.

"One day, I had to cross a high bridge, higher than any bridge I'd even seen before. I was pulling trucks loaded with important supplies so I decided **I must be brave!** I did it, even though I was scared."

Percy listened in awe as Gator finished his story.

"So you see being brave isn't the same as not feeling scared," he continued. "Being brave is about what you do even when you *do* feel scared."

Percy pulled into Knapford Station feeling much better. He told Thomas about Gator's advice. "I've decided to be brave and take the Mail Train tonight!" he said.

"Be careful out there! Monsters are hard to see in the **dark**!" cried James, pulling out of the station. He was in a bad mood because he had to pull the Flying Kipper to deliver fish that night.

Suddenly Gator came round a bend. James was so **frightened** that he missed a red signal, came off the rails and **splashed** into a pond!

"Oh, James!" chuckled Percy. "I see you've met Gator."

The other engines thought what had happened to James was very funny. "You're meant to deliver the fish, not throw them back in the water!" teased Henry.

"I'll show them who the scaredy engine is!" cried James, as the other engines left. He had a plan to scare Percy.

That night when Percy set out to take the Mail Train he came face to face with **something very strange** . . . and this time it wasn't a haystack! Percy was terrified as the strange shape shook and waved about, looming over him with its sharp spiky teeth and **long scary claws!**

CHAPTER 3

Percy raced back to the Sheds **screaming**, "The monster! The monster!" But the other engines didn't believe him.

"Silly Percy! There's no such thing as monsters. You probably saw another haystack," said James, laughing.

"I know what I saw!" said Percy, still **shaking** with fear.

The next morning Percy met Gator on the branch line.

"Where are you off to this morning?" Gator asked cheerfully.

"I'm just delivering the mail from last night . . . but maybe I should travel with you. I bet you'd know what to do if we see any monsters!" Percy felt brave with Gator by his side. "It's good to have a new friend on the Island. I'm really glad you're not going away," Percy said.

"I am going away. I've just been **useful** while I was waiting for my ship – it's coming in tonight!"

Percy was very sad.

Meanwhile, Thomas found James pushing a truck piled high with scrap.

"James! What is that?" asked Thomas.

"Nothing," said James. "It's just some **scrap** that was left on the line."

Thomas realised what James had done. "You played a trick on Percy! You made a monster out of scrap to give him a **fright**. Percy is your friend. You need to find him and say sorry!"

Thomas pulled into Knapford Station to speak to Percy. "I'm sorry about last night, Percy," Thomas said.

"I thought you were my friend," said Percy, **sadly**. "When I told you about the monster you should have believed me!"

"But Percy . . . "

"Maybe I should go to a **faraway land** and make new friends . . . like Gator," said Percy. "You can stay here on Sodor with the monsters!" And he **puffed** away before Thomas could tell him about James' monster trick.

Thomas was worried when Percy still hadn't come back later that **night**.

"Where is he?" cried Thomas.

"He started talking about doing something brave," said James.

"Perhaps I should go and look for him," Thomas said to The Fat Controller.

"Perhaps, Thomas, you should take the Mail Train for your friend," replied The Fat Controller, **angrily**. "And if you do see Percy tell him I would like to speak to him!"

Thomas pulled out of the Sheds and set off.

Meanwhile, down at the Docks, Percy was being loaded onto a **big ship** next to Gator. "Percy!" Gator cried. "What are you doing here?"

"I'm going to work in a faraway land! And show everyone how brave I can be, just like you!" said Percy.

"Well . . . **running away** from your problems is not very brave, Percy," said Gator.

When Thomas got back to the Engine Sheds after delivering the mail Percy still wasn't there. "James! Where is Percy?" cried Thomas.

"Maybe he's gone to catch a monster!" grumbled James.

"We'd better find him before he gets into trouble!" Thomas backed up and headed for the Clay Pits. But then he heard the ship's horn. He **screeched** to a halt, remembering what Percy had said about going to a faraway land. "James! Wait!" cried Thomas. But James was already too far ahead to hear him. Thomas **raced** to the Docks.

The big ship was already starting to leave.

"Stop the ship, Cranky!" shouted Thomas. "This is an **emergency**!"

Thinking quickly, Cranky swung around and caught the hull of the ship with his hook. Cranky started to bend as the great bulk of the ship threatened to pull him off the dock. Luckily the captain was able to stop the ship before Cranky was pulled into the water!

"Percy! You can't leave!" Thomas called up to the ship.

"Is that what all this is about?" Cranky asked. "I unloaded Percy half an hour ago!"

Thomas was **shocked**. "You unloaded Percy? Then . . . where is he now?"

CHAPTER 4

Percy was on his way to the Clay Pits. He thought if he could find the footprints that Thomas saw then they would prove the monster was real! Percy stopped at the danger signs.

"**Hello, scaredy engine!**" said James, who had pulled up beside Percy.

"I'm braver than you'll ever be, James!" Percy cried.

"Then why don't you keep going and look for the monster?" teased James. "Let's see who is really the **bravest**, shall we?" James pulled past the sign and headed down the track.

"Oh, monster! Come out, come out, wherever you are!" cried James.

"This is not a good idea!" said Percy, unhappily following James down the track. "That's just what I'd expect a scaredy engine to say!" **chuckled** James. But as James **chuffed** along the track some rocks tumbled down from above. Percy looked up at the crumbling wall. He moved out of the way just before a huge rock landed right in front of him with a loud **crunch**!

"Thomas was right!" gasped James. The rock had very big footprints on it!

James carried on up through the ravine by himself. There was something poking out of the rocks up ahead. More earth moved on the cliffs and crumbled away revealing a **claw**!

"**The monster!**" screamed James. He hurtled back down the track towards Percy. Frightened, Percy started to reverse quickly too, and then his eyes went wide and he **screeched** to a stop again. "No, James! Go forward! There's a landslide!"

Percy **slammed** into the back of James to force him forward again. "Go forward!" he cried.

James was directly under the path of the falling earth. As the wall collapsed behind him, James suddenly realised what was happening. He started to rush forward and Percy followed, moving close behind him as the rocks **crashed** down. A wave of earth **swept** Percy off the track and into the ravine. James was safe. He met Marion coming in from the other side.

Percy was very scared when he saw the head of the monster sliding down the slope towards him. He shut his eyes tight. Just as the teeth were about to reach him the head came to a stop – caught in Marion's shovel! Percy opened his eyes again and blinked, surprised.

"Uh?" said Percy, confused. "That's not a monster – it's a rock!"

"No, it's a fossil," explained Marion. "When something is buried for millions of years it turns into stone. This is a rock formed from the bones of a **dinosaur!**"

Later, James and Thomas went to visit Percy at the Steamworks where he was being repaired.

"I'm sorry," began James. "I played a trick on you and made a scrap monster to scare you. I'm so sorry, Percy."

"And I'm sorry too," Thomas joined in. "I should have believed you when you told me about the monster. I hope we're still friends."

"Of course we are!" said Percy, cheerfully. All the engines **peeped** their whistles with joy!

Thomas and Percy went to see the complete **Megasaurus** skeleton on display outside the Town Hall. it was amazing. Everyone had gathered to see it.

The Fat Controller stepped up to a platform. "Ladies and gentlemen, engines and coaches," he announced. "We come here today to celebrate a very brave engine. Percy could have left James to save himself, but instead, Percy pushed an engine much larger than himself to safety."

Suddenly, Emily came racing towards them. "Thomas! Percy!" she whispered urgently. "Gator is leaving."

"And that's why Percy is not just a Really Useful Fossil Hunter," continued The Fat Controller. "But one of the bravest engines on the Island of . . ." He turned to look at Percy, but he was nowhere to be seen. "Fizzling fireboxes! Where's he gone now?"

Down at the Docks, Gator was being lifted onto a big ship. Suddenly he heard a steam whistle. He looked and saw Percy racing down the Docks towards him.

"I wanted to say **goodbye** . . . and to thank you for being such a good friend," said Percy. "And for helping me learn that I could be brave."

"You helped me too, Percy!" Gator said. "Now I've seen how brave you've been, well, I think I'm ready for the highest of high bridges! But I'll miss you."

"I'll miss you too. Have a safe journey. Goodbye, Gator!"

Percy was sad to say goodbye to his new friend, but he was happy that he had his old friends beside him. "I guess you have to be brave to say goodbye to someone."

"VERY brave! I was amazed by what you did at the Clay Pits," said James. "What about if you saw a real dinosaur, Percy?"

"Percy'd blow his whistle and scare it away!" cheered Thomas.

"Really? I think I might be too scared," admitted James.

"Me too, actually," said Percy. "If I saw a real live dinosaur. They were pretty big!"

"Me three!" said Thomas. The three friends laughed as they chuffed away together.